# God Found Us You

By Lisa Tawn Bergren
Art by Laura J. Bryant

Harper BLESSINGS
HarperCollins Publishers

HarperBlessings
HarperCollins*Publishers*

God Found Us You
Text copyright © 2009 by Lisa Tawn Bergren
Illustrations copyright © 2009 by Laura J. Bryant

Manufactured in China.

Library of Congress Cataloging-in-Publication Data
Bergren, Lisa Tawn.
    God found us you / by Lisa Tawn Bergren ; art by Laura J. Bryant.
        p.     cm. — (HarperBlessings)
    Summary: When Little Fox asks his mother to tell his favorite story, Mama Fox recounts the day he arrived
in her life, from God to her arms.
    ISBN 978-0-06-113176-9 (trade bdg.)
    [1. Foxes—Fiction.  2. Adoption—Fiction.  3. Christian life—Fiction.]  I. Bryant, Laura J., ill.  II. Title.
PZ7.B452233Gf  2009                                           2008016216
[E]—dc22                                                   CIP
                                                                  AC

Typography by Jeanne L. Hogle
11  12  13  SCP  10  9  8

First Edition

To Shari, Traci, and Laura's precious, adopted children—
Eugenia, Jem, Nathan, and Elijah—and to their mothers,
who helped me make this book sing.
—L.T.B.


To Rufus and Boogie
—L.J.B.

**L**ittle Fox cuddled up to
Mama Fox one night
and said sleepily, "Mama,
tell me again about the day
I came home."

"Oh, yes," Mama said with a smile. "That is my favorite
story of all. When God found us you, it made me the
happiest mother in the world."

"Just by comin' home?" Little Fox asked with a yawn.

"Especially by coming home," Mama said.

"For so long, I dreamed of you," she said, snuggling closer.
"'Bout me?"

"About you. I dreamed of how you would look, smell, even what you would sound like. And every day I thought of how wonderful it would be to hold you in my arms."

"I started seeing you everywhere, in the leaves of the giant oak and in the bark of the pine. Even in the stars! Oh, how I longed for the day that you would arrive, when God would find us you."

"And then I came?"

"Oh, no. No matter how much I prayed it would happen, I still had to wait."

"You waited and waited and waited?"

"And *waited*. But I knew that someday you'd arrive, when God would find us you."

"It made it hard to see other mamas with their children," she said, like she was telling a secret.

"*You* were lonely for *me?*"

"Very. I could not wait until the day you'd come, the day when God would find us you."

"I'd go up to the cliffs
and watch for you. I stood
there day . . .

"After day . . .

"After day."

"Did you ever want to give up?"
Little Fox asked.

"Sometimes," Mama said, rubbing
Little Fox's cheek with hers. "But I
trusted that God knew you, and knew
me, and knew when we'd fit perfectly
together."

Little Fox paused. "How come I couldn't stay with the mother who had me?"

"She must have had very big reasons to give you up. She must have thought it was best for you."

"Did she have fur like mine? Eyes like mine?"

"Most likely." Mama smiled softly. "She must have been as beautiful as you are handsome."

"I think she prayed like crazy that you would be safe, Little Fox. I think she prayed for me as much as I prayed for her." Mama's voice got all whispery. "And God answered both our prayers."

"I came then? To you?"

Mama nodded, happy tears in her eyes. "You came then. When God found us you, you made me the happiest mama in the world."

Little Fox smiled and then thought for a moment.
"Mama, will *you* be my forever mama?"

"Always and forever. No matter what," she promised. "This is where you belong. Here, with me, my sweet child. You are mine. The best gift in the whole wide world. I will always love you and treasure you and celebrate the day you came, the day that God found us you."

Mama Fox tucked Little Fox into bed and he giggled through her last kisses. They said their prayers and whispered, "Nighty night," just like they always did.

Little Fox was glad that he had a cozy home and good food and a mama who loved him very, very much. And he went to sleep dreaming about the day he came to the big woods . . .

and first smelled his mama . . .
and knew he was loved . . .
and finally was *home*.

"When God found us you," Mama Fox
whispered in his dreams, "you made me the
happiest mama in the world."